DO

CW00482142

CONFESSION

CONFESSIONS

JEREMY MILLAR

BOOK WORKS

To Karen,
and the much abused
Jean-Jacques.

I have resolved on an enterprise
which has no precedent
and which, once complete,
will have no imitator.

This was not my first time in Italy. Some years earlier, when I was still in my youth, I made a pleasant journey across the Alps on my way to Turin. My companion, a M. Sabran, was not quite the oaf which he appeared, and which I expected him to be. He was middle-aged with a big mouth, and wore his greying black hair in a pony-tail. It wasn't quite clear why he was travelling, although it seemed that he had an idea for establishing some kind of manufacturers in Annecy and was now making the jouney to Turin to try and get the minister's consent. I'm not sure what he intended to manufacture as he seemed to be a jack of all trades without being a master of any of them. He was certainly an intriguing man, and never failed to become friendly with any priest whom we happened, not altogether accidentally, to come across. He had learnt a kind of religious jargon in school, which he never failed to make use of, and repeated the one passage which he knew from the Latin Bible at least a thousand times a day. And he was seldom short of money, especially if he knew that someone else had some upon them.

His wife, Mme Sabran, was also decent enough, although she tended to be rather quieter during the day than she was at night. As I had to share their room, her noisy sleeplessness woke me constantly, and would have done even more frequently if I had at that time known the reason for it. As it was, I would have to wait a little longer until I was to lose my ignorance.

And so I walked happily with my guide and his energetic companion. Nothing troubled my journey and I was as happy mentally and physically as I had been at any time in my life. I was young and enthusiastic, healthy and vigorous, enjoying to the full the richness of my life and the world around me. Everything I saw seemed to me a guarantee of my future happiness. Every house became a place of rest and country feasts, every river a source of bathing and endless fish. Fruit appeared on every tree; and below, a shaded spot in which to rest. I was enjoying the quiet simplicity of idleness, the pure joy of wandering aimlessly, and nowhere did I turn my eyes without being struck by the beauty of it all. The memories of this time have left me with a strong desire for everything that I associate with it, for travelling on foot and for mountains especially. As we had to slow our pace to that of Mme Sabran, this seven or eight day stroll was the only period of my life that I can remember that was completely free from any sort of care or anxiety.

Of course, I was disappointed finally to reach Turin, although this soon faded as I realised the size of the town and thought to my hopes for creating a name worthy of myself there. Ambition was now filling my head, and already I thought of myself as far superior to the boy that started the journey, although I didn't realise that there were plenty of opportunities here to fall far below that level.

When I arrived, I presented my letters of intro-duction and was immediately taken to the hospice for converts, which was the goal of my journey, to be in-structed in the faith which was to be my keep. I had an intimidating beginning, as a huge iron-barred door was hanged shut behind me and double-locked. This gave me plenty to think about, even before I was shown to a room, of considerable size, which was empty except for a wooden altar, at the far end, with a large crucifix upon it and four or five wooden chairs scattered round the walls. There, in this assembly-hall were four or five of my fellow pupils, who looked more like the devil's body-guards than those who aspired to become the children of God. Two of them, who were Croats, freely admitted to me that they spent most of their time roaming through Spain and Italy, embracing Christianity and being bap-tised wherever the rewards made it worthwhile. Just then another iron door was opened half-way along a balcony overlooking the courtyard and through it entered our sister-converts. They were the biggest bunch of god-forsaken sluts that you have ever seen! Only one of them seemed quite attractive, and she was perhaps a year or so older than myself, her eye often catching mine, which made me want to become better acquainted. Unfortu-nately, it was impossible for me to get nearer to her as she was closely watched by her gaoleress and the holy missioner, who worked with enthusiasm, if not success, towards her conversion.

This small community was gathered together in honour of my arrival. There was a small speech, encouraging me to take full advantage of the situation in which I now found myself, and inviting the others to help me on my way and to lead me by their examples. After that, the virgins were returned to their cloister, and I was left alone to wonder at this strange place.

I never exactly decided to become Catholic, but seeing that my conversion was approaching, I tried to accustom myself to the idea as best I could, while at the same time, trying to imagine some unusual event which might rescue me from my predicament. I decided to try to delay their activities for as long as I could, and as soon as I could see that it was possible to confuse those who were trying to instruct me, I put all my energies into this activity, working on them as they were working upon me. Eventually I believed, in the arrogance of youth, that I only had to persuade them and they would become Protestants! I won't comment as to my success in this project although they certainly found me more difficult than they expected. They knew also that Protestants are generally better educated in such matters than Catholics as their faith requires discussion rather than submission, but I am sure that they did not expect that I would present any great difficulties to men of their age and experience, given that I was lacking in both.

The next day we were collected all together for the first lesson, which was given by a little old priest. For my companions, the problem was being taught, not being convinced. I was a little more difficult, however. I decided to hold the priest up at each and every point, which made the lesson a very long one and which bored the rest of the pupils no end. The old priest became flustered and kept drifting from the point in hand, eventually getting out of the problem by saying that he didn't understand my language very well. Of course, the next day I had a lesson all by myself, so that the others would not be upset. I now had a younger priest who was a very good talker, by which I mean he used extremely long words in his extremely long sentences. I refused to be intimidated by his manner however, and I began to answer him with an assurance which was greater than my years and indeed my knowledge. He threw Saint Augustine, Saint Gregory and all the other Fathers my way but to his utter surprise, I could handle them as well as he could and proceeded to throw them back to him! I took pleasure in these meetings although, in the end, I was forced to concede for two reasons. The first was because he was stronger than myself, and knowing that I was more or less at his mercy, even in my youth I had sufficient judgement not push him too far, as I could see by the reaction of the old priest that it would get me nowhere. The second reason was simply that the young priest had studied a great deal and I had not. He knew how to structure arguments so as to confuse me, to deny the authenticity of my quotations and even, when I presented him with a difficult objection, to postpone the lesson until the next day, saying that I was straying too far from the point in hand. In the end, I rather suspected him of resorting to the sorts of discursive trickery of which he accused Protestant ministers, and of simply inventing passages which suited him.

It was during these petty arguments, while I was wasting my time in word-play and prayers, that I had an extremely unpleasant experience which, in the end, could have been much worse. There is no heart so dark as to be immune to some sort of affection, and one of the thugs at the hospice began to take a fancy to me. He often came up to me and gossiped, talking to me in his strange way, sometimes giving me pieces of his food at the table and frequently kissing me with a strength that I found unpleasant. Though I was frightened, naturally, by his rough, dark face and the passion of his glances, I put up with his approaches, saying to myself, 'The poor man has conceived a warm friendship for me; it would be wrong to repulse him.' But his approaches became stronger, and his suggestions became so strange that I thought that there must be something wrong with him. One night he wanted to share my bed but I refused, saying it was too small, whereupon he tried to get me to come into his. I refused, however, as he was so dirty and stank so much of the tobacco that he constantly chewed that I thought that I would be ill.

The next day, very early in the morning, we found ourselves alone in the assembly hall. He resumed his caresses, but now with such a force that I started to become worried. He tried to take advantage of me and, by guiding my hand towards him, to make me do the same things. I broke free from his clutches with a cry;

although I had no idea what was happening, my suprise and disgust were so visible that he then left me alone. But as he let me go, I saw something white and sticky shoot from him towards the fireplace and fall upon the ground. My stomach turned and I rushed onto the balcony more upset than I had ever been in my life. I was nearly sick.

Nevertheless, I couldn't work out what was wrong with the man. He seemed to be caught in an epileptic fit. In all my life I have never seen a more revolting sight than the hideousness of a face screwed up by the workings of lust. Fortunately, I have not seen another man in this same state, but if this is how we appear to women, then they must indeed find us fascinating in order not to find us revolting.

My mind was confused and I could think of nothing better to do than go to tell the others what had just happened. The old woman told me to keep quiet although I could see that my story had upset her as she kept muttering under her breath: *Can maledet! brutta bestia!* I didn't see why I should keep quiet so I carried on telling my story. In fact, I talked so much that the next day one of the principals came to me very early in the morning and gave a sharp lecture, accusing me of attempting to destroy the fine reputation of the establishment and of making something out of nothing. In addition to this, he told me a number of things of which I was ignorant but which I do not think the priest suspected he was explaining for the first time. He thought that I knew what the man wanted from me but that I was merely unwilling. He told me that the act which the man had desired was forbidden and immoral, but that such desire was not intended as an insult to the person who was the object of that desire. There was nothing to get worried about in being found attractive. Indeed, the priest told me frankly, he had been found so in his youth and in a position similar to mine, where he could put up less resistance, had found nothing so wrong about the whole business. He went on to describe the whole thing in such clear terms, using such frank terminology, that I felt uneasy. He even went as far as to reassure me that if the reason for my refusal had been the pain which I might have been caused, then my concerns were unfounded. There was nothing to worry about.

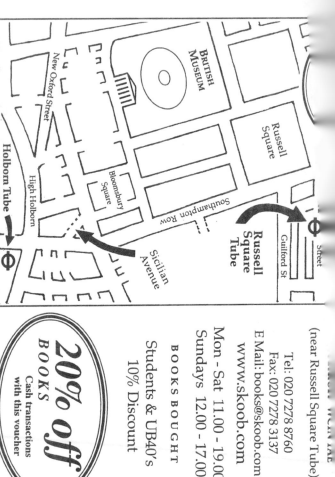

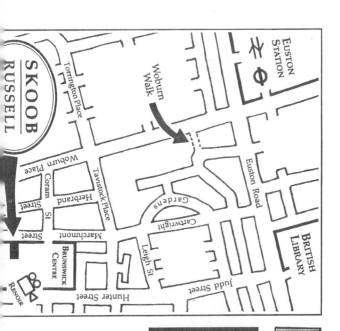

SKOOBOOKS

SPECIAL OFFER

**SKOOB
RUSSELL
SQUARE**

10 Brunswick Centre
off Bernard Street
London WC1N

I couldn't believe my ears, especially as he was trying to instruct me for my own good! The whole thing seemed so straightforward to him that he didn't even find any privacy for our discussion and we were listened to the whole time by an ecclesiastic who seemed to find the incident quite usual. The situation was such that in the end I believed that this behaviour was normal practice in the world, and that this was simply the first time that I had come across it, so to speak. So, I listened without any trace of anger although the memory of what I had seen meant that I was unable to listen without disgust. I began to associate the whole sordid affair with the man who was now the apologist for it, and as I could not hide my feelings for the event or for him, from then on he spared me nothing that would make my stay there any more unpleasant than it was already. He succeded in his task and I saw before me only one way of escape. From then on, I made as much effort to take it as I had previously taken in avoiding it.

These events made me wary in the future against the attentions of such men. The sight of people who possess such a reputation, which reminded me of the looks and behaviour of that frightful man, always horrified me to such an extent that I found it difficult to hide my disgust. On the other hand, women became more valuable to me, by way of contrast. I felt as though I owed them for the offences of all men, something which I could only put right by the most delicate of affections. My own memories of that forceful African transformed the most repulsive of sluts into the most wondrous object of adoration.

I did not have to put up with his glances for long as a week later he was baptised with great ceremony, draped in white in a misguided attempt to symbolise the purity of his newly cleansed soul. The next day he left the hospice and I never saw him again. My turn came about a month later. Of course the directors made a big show of my conversion, glorying in a difficult triumph, and eventually spared no detail of Catholic pomp and ceremony that would make the event any less solemn for the public or any less humiliating for me. The only thing that was missing was a white robe, which I would have found useful later, but which I was denied because unlike the Moor, I didn't have the honour of being a Jew.

When the whole thing was over and I was waiting to be given the post which I had been expecting, I was turned out of the door with little more than some loose change, the result of the collection. They encouraged me to live the life of a good Christian, wished me luck and then disappeared behind a closed door.

I knew sufficient Italian by now to make myself understood and it did not take long for me to find a lodging. My reasoning was more dependent upon my purse than my taste and consequently I decided upon a bed at a soldier's wife's in Via di Po, which was cheap at least. She was young and recently married, although she already had five or six children. All of us, mother, children and lodgers shared a room, and things went on all the time that I was staying there. She swore like a trooper and was generally pretty scruffy but all in all, she was a good woman, kind-hearted and obliging, and even did me a favour. One day she informed me that she had found me a position and that the lady, Countess de Vercellis, wanted to see me. This news really made me think that this was the start of something big for me, something which my mind was always half expecting.

But in the end, it was not as exciting as I had hoped or even expected. I went to the house with the servant who had mentioned me to the Countess, and as I seemed to pass her short examination, I entered her service on the spot. Unfortunately, I did not become her favourite, but merely a valet, and dressed in her servants' uniform, or in fact, an even plainer version of it!

The three months that I remained in her service were unremarkable, and although I received no formal education, there are a couple of things which I learnt in this period which I would like to relate here. The Countess de Vercellis was a childless widow, of middle years and a distinguished appearance, who came originally from Savoie. She possessed a cultured mind and was extremely fond of French literature, a subject about which she was well informed. Her letters, of which she wrote a great number and always in French, never failed to display a high degree of character and grace. My principal occupation, which I therefore found a pleasure, was to write down her letters from her dictation, as unfortunately she also suffered from breast cancer, which caused her great pain and which prevented her from writing herself.

My first lesson was to observe the malicious intrigue which surrounded her demise with all those who sought to profit from it. Her nephew, the Count de la Roque, was her heir, and his attentions became noticeably more concerned as time passed. So too were those of her servants, who did not forget their own interests; at the end, she had so many devoted attendants that she hardly had time to think of me. Chief amongst these was the head of the household, a certain M. Lorenzi, a clever man whose even cleverer wife had so successfully wormed her way into the lady's favour that she lived more as a friend than a paid servant. She had also successfully placed her niece, Mlle Pontal, as the lady's maid, and she proved to be as manipulative and as scheming as the rest of her family. Through their close attentions, the Countess only saw through their eyes and only acted through their hands, a sorry state of affairs, but one which prepared me, if only a little, for my later stay in Venice. Their greed prevented them from being just and they saw any monies left to others as coming out of the property which they already owned. They joined together to prevent me entering her sight, even to the extent that they persuaded her doctor to make her give up letter writing, which was her sole remaining pleasure, on the pretence that it was too tiring for her. As it was, I did not see her once in the week before she made her will, although I was left to look after her continuously afterwards. Indeed, if I learned a lot about the frailties of the human soul from those that surrounded the Countess, I learned even more about its strength from her, although she was physically the weakest of us all. It was true that she could often be harsh, and when she performed a kindness it usually had more to do with principle than any true sense of compassion. Nevertheless, the fortitude with which she bore her suffering inspired in me nothing but the greatest respect and affection for her.

In the end I watched her die, and she died like a philosopher. With the serenity of heart with which she fulfilled her instructions, she made my newly found faith, the Catholic religion, seem beautiful to me. Although she was generally of a serious nature, towards the end of her life she displayed a humour which was too sustained to be anything other than genuine. She only stayed in bed for the last two days, and there she continued to talk quietly and carefully till the last. Finally, in the middle of her death agonies, she broke wind loudly. 'Good,' she said, turning over, 'a woman who can fart is not dead.' And those were her last words.

Apart from those lessons which I had taken from the events surrounding the death of the Countess, I left the house much as I had entered it. I went back to my old landlady and stayed with her for about five or six weeks, during which time a combination of my health, my age and my idleness began to have a disturbing effect upon my feelings. I often felt distant and lost, restless and absent-minded. I longed for a pleasure which I felt I lacked although I certainly could not imagine what it could be. The state was indescribable and unbearable; and I doubt that you can even imagine it. Most of you will have experienced this delicious torment as simply an intoxication of desire, which at least gives one a foretaste of its own gratification. The heat of my blood constantly filled my head with images of girls, but not knowing the true nature of sex, I imagined them acting only as my own strange fantasies dictated, and while these kept my senses and my body in a state of frenzied activity, they did not teach me to relieve myself. Shame, which accompanies the workings of a dark conscience, had increased with my years, an event which only intensified my own natural shyness. Indeed, neither at that time or since, have I possessed the courage to make a sexual advance to any woman who has not more or less forced me to do so, even when I knew her history and was unlikely to be refused.

My mind became so disturbed that being unable to either control or satisfy my desires, I began to excite them by the most extravagant means. I hid in dark alleys and secluded spots where I could expose myself to women from a distance, in the state of undress in which I should like to have been in their company. I did not think that what they saw was obscene, but simply ridiculous. I cannot describe the strange pleasure which I received from displaying myself before them. I was only one step away from the experience which I desired, and I have no doubt that some bold girl would have pleased me, as she passed, if I had had the courage to wait. But these strange events led to a near catastrophe which was almost equally ridiculous, although rather less enjoyable on my part.

One day I took up my position in the corner of a courtyard where I knew that the girls of the house often came to meet. Down in this corner were some steps which led to some cellars which I explored in the dark and which, seeing as they seemed to go on forever, I decided it would be an ideal hiding place should I need it. With the safety of this retreat in mind, I gave the assembled girls a sight which was more comical than seductive. Some of them started laughing, others became insulted and made a fuss while the rest pretended that they had seen nothing, which may indeed have been the case. I turned and hurried into my retreat, hearing footsteps behind me. Then I heard the voice of a man behind me – which I had certainly not expected – and which sent me alarmed, deeper and deeper into the dark passages. But still the footsteps, the noises and the voices, especially the man's, followed me. My plan depended on the dark but now it was becoming light. Shuddering, I carried on until, faced with a wall, I was forced to stop. I didn't have to wait long as almost before I had noticed, a big man with a big moustache, a big hat and a big knife grabbed me. Behind him were four or five woman, each armed with broomhandles; and the little tart who had no doubt given me away in the first place. The man with the knife seized my arm and asked me, angrily, what I was doing there. Obviously, I didn't really have an explanation to hand, but I tried to collect my thoughts and with the greatest mental exertions, I managed to produce a somewhat romantic excuse which, surprisingly, was accepted. I asked him, in the softest, most pleading terms, to excuse my behaviour, claiming that I had fallen from a noble birth and was suffering from a strange mental condition! I added that I had run away from my family as they wanted to lock me away and that if he reported me then I would suffer terribly but that if he let me off, I should one day repay his kindness. Unbelieveable, I know, but my speech semed to have the desired effect and the poor man was touched! He gave me a brief telling-off but let me go without any further questions and certainly no further punishment. From the looks I received from the women and that girl, I

could see that the man of whom I had been so frightened
had, in fact, saved me and that if I had been caught by
them, I should have come off a lot worse. They started
muttering but I didn't pay much attention because I
knew that as long as the man and his knife didn't interfere with me, I could probably escape from their attentions without too much difficulty.

About a week later, as I walked down the street with
a young abbé who lived close by, I came across the man
with the knife. Of course, he recognised me and in a
high-pitched imitation of my voice, he mocked: 'I am a
prince. I am a prince and a coward. But don't let his
Highness come back again.' I said nothing but disappeared with my head down, thanking him, in my heart
at least, for not giving me away. I suppose it was those
horrid old women who had ridiculed him for believing
me, but he was a good man, and I never think of the incident without a sense of gratitude towards him. Anyone
else would have tormented me unbearably, just to get a
laugh, so ridiculous was the whole episode. It certainly
made me more cautious in the future.

I was extremely fortunate in that these incidents, which may not have given the most generous impression of myself, did not have the consequences which I may have feared. They certainly did not seem to have an effect upon my appointment in Venice, which I shall now relate, although I am sure that this has more to do with those concerned being ignorant of the events rather than approving of them.

It was considerably later that the Count de Montaigu, a captain in the Guards, was made the ambassador to Venice. His brother, the Chevalier de Montaigu, was the acquaintance of two friends of mine – Mme de Broglie and Mme de Beuzenval – as well as the Abbé Alary of the French Academy, whom I sometimes saw. Mme de Broglie learned that the new ambassador was in need of a secretary and so proposed me. We began to discuss the terms of my appointment although the little they offered was not enough to make me leave my home. I remained, and M. de Montaigu took a secretary which the Foreign Office had given him, a M. Follau. They didn't work together for long, for as soon as they reached Venice they argued and Follau left, saying that he couldn't deal with a madman. The ambassador was forced to turn to me to relieve him from his predicament, although it was his brother, who was far cleverer, who convinced me of the privileges which went with my position, and I left having accepted the wages that I had initially refused. Perhaps I should have paid more attention to my original judgement.

When I finally arrived in Venice, I found piles of dispatches waiting for me, from both the Court and from the other embassies. The ambassador, M. de Montaigu, had been unable to read those that were in code, even though he had all the code books that he required. As I had never worked in an office in my life, and had certainly never seen a ministerial cipher, I was a little worried at first although my concerns were unjustified, and within a week I had deciphered them all. I needn't have bothered, as not only is the Venetian embassy always pretty quiet, but the ambassador was not the sort of man whom anyone would have bothered with even the simplest problem. As he could neither dictate a letter nor write legibly, he recognised how useful I was to him and he treated me accordingly. Naturally, he had another reason for doing so. After the retirement of his predecessor (M. de Froulay, who had gone mad), the French Consul, M. Le Blond, had taken over the embassy business, which he continued to manage now that M. de Montaigu had arrived, until he had had the time to instruct the newcomer fully in his duties. Although the ambassador was unable to carry out his work, he hated the idea of anyone else doing it for him and so took a dislike to the consul. As soon as I arrived, therefore, he deprived the consul of his duties as secretary to the embassy and gave them to me, allowing me to assume the title which went with them. It was quite natural, I suppose, that the ambassador should prefer his own man as secretary to the embassy rather than someone else who had been nominated by the Court, and as long as I remained there, he never sent anyone else in a secretarial role to either the Senate or its Foreign Officer.

This made my position a relatively pleasant one, and one which prevented his gentlemen, who like his pages and the majority of his staff were Italians, from disputing my authority within the house. As a result, I was able to protect the ambassador's rights, and to prevent the many attempts that were made to break into his rooms. At the same time, I did not provide sanctuary to thieves, despite the financial benefits which I would have made, and of which no doubt his Excellency would have enjoyed a share.

He even attempted to claim part of the secretary's fees, called the chancellery dues, for himself. Although we were at war, there were no shortage of passport applications, and a small amount was paid to the secretary who drew up and countersigned each one. All my predecessors had collected this money from every person who made an application, which seemed unfair to me, and although not a Frenchman myself, I abolished the payment for the French applicants. However, I remained firm in my attempts to collect it from everyone else, to the extent that when the Marquis Scotti, the brother of the Queen of Spain's favourite, sent a messenger to demand a passport without including my payment, I sent the man back to collect it, something which that vindictive Italian did not forget. Of course, as soon as news spread of my tax reform, my only applications came from crowds of would-be Frenchmen, who, in embarrassing accents, claimed they were born in Provence, Picardy, or Burgundy. Of course, I didn't fall for any of it, and I doubt that a single Italian cheated me, or that a single Frenchman was himself cheated. However, I was stupid enough to tell M. de Montaigu what I had done, even though he would never have known about it otherwise. The word 'money' made him prick up his ears, and although he did not say a word about my abolishing the fee for the French, he demanded that we split the rest of the money, promising me that I would receive my benefits elsewhere. I was having none of it, but he didn't let up. We both got heated and I told him, 'Sir, let your Excellency keep what is yours and leave me what is mine. I will never hand over a penny to you.' He could see that he was not getting anywhere with me and in the end had the cheek to say that since I profited from the chancellery, I should pay its expenses. There was no point arguing, and from then on, I paid for the ink, paper, candles and ribbon, even the seal, which I had repaired without ever being reimbursed. However, even these expenses did not stop me from giving some of my revenue to the Abbé de Binis, a good man who would never have asked for the money.

I found my work easier than I had dared hope, despite the inexperience both of myself and the ambassador I was working under. I'm unsure as to whether it was ignorance or otherwise, but he always seemed to manage to ruin anything that common sense and an ounce of intelligence would have shown to be in his best interests, and in those of the King. The best move he ever made was to ally himself with the Marquis de Mari, the Spanish ambassador, an intelligent, political man who could have had him do anything he wished but who, seeing the common interests of the two kingdoms, generally gave him good advice. Unfortunately, M. de Montaigu always had to spoil things by adding his own little idea when carrying out de Mari's plans. The one thing they both had to do was ensure that the Venetians remained neutral, which they continually stressed, even as they continually provided the Austrians with supplies and recruits, who posed as deserters. It seemed that M. de Montaigu wanted to keep in with the Republic and therefore, despite my protests, always made me state in all his dispatches that Venice would never violate her neutrality. At times his stubborn stupidity made my duties unbearable. For example, he absolutely insisted that the bulk of his dispatches to the King and the minister should be in code, although this was totally unnecessary. I argued that there was not enough time to do all the ciphering, and also deal with the heavy correspondence, between the Friday, when dispatches arrived from Court, and Saturday, when ours were sent off. His idea was inspired – to write the replies on Thursday to the dispatches which would arrive the next day. My complaints may seem obvious to others, but he was so taken by the ingenuity of his idea that I was forced to concede. This meant that all week long, I would keep note of some of his odd mutterings and of trivial news stories which I picked up here and there. Then, armed with this flimsy material, I would bring him a rough draft of the dispatch on Thursday morning, and would make certain additions in light of the dispatches we received on Friday, to which ours were supposed to be a reply.

He had another strange habit, which also made his correspondences unimaginably absurd, which was to send each news item back to its source instead of passing it on. He reported Court news to M. Amelot, news from Paris to M. de Maurepas, from Sweden to M. d'Havrincourt and from Petersburg to M. de la Chetardie. Fortunately, as he only looked at those dispatches for the Court, and signed the rest unread, I was able to change the others, passing on the information which they contained. I was lucky if he didn't want to add some lines of his own, which meant that I had to go back and write out the whole thing to include his own irrelevance, and put it in code, or he would not have signed it. I was often tempted to cipher something different from what he had said, simply for the sake of his reputation, but nothing could justify this breach of faith and I let him go on as he liked, satisfied that I was only doing my duty.

I feel proud of the fact that I accomplished my duties with an honesty, an enthusiasm and a courage which deserved a better reward than that which I received. I was alone, without friends, advice or experience, in a foreign land, and in foreign service, surrounded by undesirables who, for their own interests and in order to prevent themselves being shown up by my example, urged me to do as they did. Of course, I refused and served France well although I owed her nothing, and did my duty to her ambassador, as far as things depended upon me. In a position fully open to scrutiny, I deservedly won the respect of the Republic and of all the ambassadors with whom we were in contact, as well as the affection of all the French residents in Venice, including the consul, whose duties I had been given, something which often caused me embarrassment and regret.

Being totally under the control of the Marquis de Mari, who did not worry about the details of his duties, M. de Montaigu so neglected his that, if it were not for my efforts, the French in Venice would have thought themselves without an ambassador. He always dismissed them without a hearing when they asked for his help so that, before long, they became so disgusted with him that they would not have appeared at his table, even if he had indeed invited them (which, of course, he never did). I adopted his responsibilities as my own, and did everything in my power to help any Frenchman who approached the embassy with some need or other. In any other country I could have done more, but as I was in too humble a position to see anyone in authority, I often had to turn to the consul who, having established himself and his family there, was forced to act differently from the way in which he would have liked. Sometimes, when I saw this happening, I took his steps for him, which often succeeded. One incident still makes me laugh. You wouldn't have guessed that, if it hadn't been for me, Parisian theatre-goers would have been deprived of Coralline and her sister Camille, but I assure you it's true. Their father, Veronese, had signed a contract for himself and his daughters with the Italian company but, after receiving two thousand francs for travelling expenses had not set out. Instead they had appeared at the Teatro di San Luca in Venice, where Coralline, though just a child, was drawing a crowd. The Duc de Gesvres, as lord chamberlain, wrote to the ambassador, claiming the family although when he received the letter, M. de Montaigu merely handed it to me and said, 'Look into that.' I went to M. Le Blond and asked him to speak to the owner of the theatre – one of the Giustiniani –

and persuade him to dismiss Veronese, since he was under contract to the King. The consul didn't really fancy the job and did it badly, Giustiniani making some stupid excuse and hanging on to Veronese. Of course, I was annoyed. As it was carnival time, I took a domino and a mask and set out for the Palazzo Giustiniani. When my gondola, complete with the ambassador's livery, arrived at the Palazzo, everyone was impressed. I had myself announced as *una siora maschera*, but once inside I took off my mask and announced my name. The senator stood pale and speechless. 'Sir,' I said to him in the Venetian dialect, 'I am sorry to trouble your excellency by my visit; but you have at your Teatro di San Luca a man named Veronese, who is under contract to the King. He has been claimed from you, but without success. I have come to ask for him in His Majesty's name.' My speech was effective. The moment I left, he hurriedly gave an account of the incident to the State Inquisitors, who gave him a severe talking-to. Veronese was dismissed the same day, and I sent him a message saying that if he didn't leave within a week I would have him arrested. And of course, he left.

Another occasion was when I got the skipper of a merchant vessel out of trouble, almost single-handedly. I can't remember the name of the ship, but he was Captain Olivet from Marseilles. His crew had got into a fight with some Slavonians in the State service and as a result, no one except the captain could board or leave the ship without permission. Of course, the ambassador sent him packing, while the consul remarked that it was a commercial affair and as such, he could not interfere. I mentioned to M. de Montaigu that he should allow me to make a statement about the affair before the Senate and although I cannot remember whether I did or not, I know that the embargo remained and that I was forced to take another course of action. I knew that our dispatches were opened and read in Venice, although they contained nothing which was worth the trouble (I knew this because I often found articles reproduced word for word in the *Gazette*, something which I tried in vain to get the ambassador to complain about). I decided to use this fact to my advantage and, after much discussion, managed to persuade M. de Montaigu to let me mention the incident in a dispatch to M. de Maurepas. I hoped that when the Venetians read the report, which I was certain they would, they would give the vessel up before we had to wait for a reply from the Court, by which time the captain would be ruined. But this was not all. I went also to visit the ship in order to question the crew, taking with me the reluctant Abbé Patizel, chancellor of the consulate, who was scared of offending the Senate. As I was not allowed to enter the ship, I drew my gondola alongside and there made my interrogation, questioning every man in the crew, one by one, in a loud voice and in such a way as to allow them to reply favourably. I tried to persuade Abbé Patizel to ask the questions and to draw up the interrogatory, something he was better at than myself, but he absolutely refused, scarcely uttered a word and almost refused to sign the interrogatory after me. Despite this reluctance, my daring plan worked, and the ship was released long before we received a reply from the ministry. The captain wanted to give me a present, to show his gratitude for my bold actions, but I simply slapped him on the shoulder and said, 'Captain Olivet, do you think that a man who does not ask Frenchmen for passport fees, which are his established right, is a man

who takes payment for affording the King's protection?'
He wanted, at least, to give me dinner on board, which
I accepted, and to which I took Carrio, a talented and
charming man who was the secretary to the Spanish embassy and who has since become secretary to the Paris
embassy and chargé d'affaires.

I would have been happier if, while I carried out
my good works, I had been able to organise the running
of the office so that I was not carrying out my duties at
my own expense. However, as I was in such a junior position, even the smallest mistakes were not without their
consequences and, as a result, I paid most of my attention avoiding such errors. Apart from the odd mistake I
made in ciphering the dispatches, which had more to
do with the necessary haste with which they had to be
produced and which M. Amelot's clerks complained
about on only one occassion, neither the ambassador
nor anyone else ever complained about any signs of
negligence in my duties, which is remarkable given how
negligent I often am. But sometimes I was careless and
forgetful in the special projects which I sometimes
undertook, and my innate sense of judgement has always

made me take the blame for my actions before anyone had even thought of complaining about me. I will only mention one incident, which is connected to my leaving Venice, and which later gave me problems in Paris.

Our cook, a man named Rousselot, had brought a bill from a wig-maker acquaintance of his in Paris for a Venetian nobleman called Gianetto Nani. Rousselot brought me the bill and asked if I could possibly get some payment for it, although it was a well known custom for Venetian nobles, once they had returned home, to refuse to pay any of the debts which they had run up abroad. When some poor soul tries to force them to pay, they delay payment so long that, in the end, he either gives up or settles for much less than he was owed. I asked M. Le Blond to speak to Gianetto, who admitted he owed the money but still refused to pay it. After much negotiation, he offered to pay a small amount but when Le Blond went to collect the money, it wasn't ready and he was told that he would have to wait. During this time, I had my argument with the ambassador and left my job. I left all the embassy papers in perfect order, but for some strange reason, Rousselot's bill just disappeared.

M. Le Blond swore that he had returned it to me, and I believed his honesty, but I had no idea what had happened to it. As Gianetto had admitted owing the money, I asked M. Le Blond if he could try to get the money from him on a receipt, or to get him to provide a duplicate bill. But once Gianetto realised what had happened, he refused to do either. I then offered Rousselot the money out of my own pocket, to clear things up, but he passed me on to the wig-maker who, knowing what had happened, demanded either his bill or the entire sum. What I would have done to have found that scrap of paper! So, although I was poor myself, I ended up paying the entire bill. As it turned out, the creditor was payed in full whereas if – unluckily for him – the bill had been found, he would have been lucky to have got anything from His Excellency Gianetto Nani.

I was good at my job and this meant that I enjoyed it; and except for my friends Carrio and Altuna, whom I'll tell you about in a minute, the delights of Piazza di San Marco and the theatre, I made my duties my sole pleasure. Although my work was pretty easy, especially as I had Abbé de Binis helping me, I was still pretty busy, since we had a lot of correspondence and it was a time of war. I worked every day for most of the morning, and on the post-days often till midnight. The ambassadors and ministers of the Crown, with whom we were in contact, often complimented the ambassador on the excellence of his secretary, which should have pleased him, but which somehow had the opposite effect. One incident, in particular, is worth describing.

Even on Saturdays, the day when nearly all the couriers left, the ambassador was so eager to leave that he kept getting me to hurry with the royal and ministerial dispatches, which he would then quickly sign before running off somewhere or other, leaving most of the letters without signatures. Often, when they just contained news, I simply turned them into bulletins; but when they related to the King's service, someone had to sign them and so that someone was often me. I was forced to do this with an important dispatch which we had received from the King's chargé d'affaires in Vienna, M. Vincent. It was around the time when Prince Lobkowitz was advancing on Naples and the Count de Gages made his memorable retreat. The dispatch said that a man, whose details were enclosed, was leaving Vienna and travelling via Venice on a secret journey into the Abruzzi, with the intention of initiating a popular uprising on the Austrians' approach. In the absence of the ambassador, who was not interested in anything, I passed the warning on to the Marquis de l'Hôpital; it arrived just in time to be useful. Perhaps it is thanks to my much abused self that the Bourbons owe the preservation of the Kingdom of Naples.

In thanking the ambassador, as was expected, the Marquis de l'Hôpital also mentioned me and my contribution to the common cause. The ambassador, who perhaps felt a sense of guilt about his negligence, thought the remark a sarcastic comment on his duties and made sure that I knew about it. I admit that I did take the opportunities that were available to make myself known, but I certainly didn't go out of my way to find them. It seemed reasonable that if I carried out my duties well, that I should receive the appropriate acknowledgement, which is the right of those in a position to judge and reward them. I can't say if my hard work gave the ambassador a legitimate cause for complaint, but I do know that it was the only one which he ever made.

He never thought of establishing any order into his house and it was always full of hangers-on. The French were badly treated and the Italians took over. Even the best of these, good men who had given years of service to the embassy, were sacked without any sort of courtesy or acknowledgement. There was one man, a low-life from Mantua called Domenico Vitali, who was chosen by the ambassador and whom he trusted with looking after the house. By the most underhand means, this man became his closest ally, much to the detriment of the few honest men remaining in the household, myself amongst them. It's certainly true that no cheat can ever face the simple glance of an honest man, and this fact alone would have been reason enough for him to hate me. But his hate was intensified by other things, which I must say now, in order that I am fairly judged.

As was the custom, the ambassador had a box at each of the five theatres, and every day at dinner he would announce which of them he intended to visit that evening. I had the second choice and the others disposed of the rest of the boxes between themselves. One day, I ordered my servant to bring me the key to the box which I had chosen. Instead of passing it on to him, as he should have done, Vitali told my servant that he had already disposed of it himself, and as if this was not bad enough, the servant informed me of Vitali's response in public. That evening, Vitali tried to offer his apologies but I refused to accept them. Instead I replied, 'Tomorrow, sir, you will come and apologise to me at such and such an hour in the house where I received the insult, and before the people who witnessed it or, on the day after, come what may, I promise you that either you or I will depart from here.' My tone seemed to impress him, and he came to the house as I ordered and offered me a public apology in the abject manner which was typical of his character. But he was slowly making his plans, and while he continued to treat me with an exaggerated respect, his typically Italian scheming was such that, although he couldn't persuade the ambassador to fire me, in the end he forced me to resign.

Of course, someone as corrupt as Vitali could not hope to understand me, although he understood enough to achieve his ends. He knew that I was good-natured and patient, especially in putting up with unavoidable problems, but that I was proud and quick to defend myself when faced with a premeditated attack. He knew also that I demanded a sense of decency and dignity when the situation required it, and that I expected the respect due to me, just as I was careful to pay respect to others, and he used this as a way of provoking me. He turned the ambassador's house upside down, ignoring all the rules and the sense of order and efficiency which I had tried to maintain. A house without a woman requires a strong sense of discipline if decency is to be preserved, and without decency there is no dignity. He soon turned the place into a haven for drunks and thieves, and in the place of one of the gentlemen which he had had fired, he brought in another pimp like himself, who ran a brothel at the sign of the Maltese Cross. In the end, it was only the ambassador's room which was fit for a gentleman, and even that is open to question.

As the ambassador did not have supper, we had a meal to ourselves in the evening, which we shared with the Abbé de Binis and the pages. The surroundings would have been cleaner and the food better if we had gone to the lowest pub. Not only that, but they also took away my gondola, and I became the only ambassadorial secretary who was forced to hire one or else go on foot. And I was only attended by his Excellency's servants when I went to the Senate. I could have put up with all the things that went on in private, but these things angered me, as did the fact that everyone in Venice knew what went on in the embassy. All the officials complained loudly, as did I to the ambassador, not only about our treatment but also of his own conduct (however, I was the only one in the house who said nothing outside). For his own evil reasons, the ambassador never failed in his daily insult towards me, and though I had to spend my money freely in order to keep up with my colleagues, and to live up to my position, I could not touch a penny of my wages. Even when I asked his Excellency for some money, he told me of his faith in my character, as though I could live off his snide comments.

So Vitali and his *amico* managed to turn the ambassador against me completely, although he seemed to think little enough of me to start with. They got him involved with all sorts of suspicious deals in antiquities, in which they invariably persuaded him that he was making a profit while in fact he was always losing out. They also got him to rent a palazzo on the Brenta for twice its value, and then split the extra with the owner. It was a beautiful building, its apartments encrusted with mosaics and held by the very finest Italian marble pillars and pilasters. But, in his wisdom, M. de Montaigu had the whole thing covered in wooden panelling, just because it is the fashion in Paris. Similarly, he was the only ambassador in the whole of Venice who deprived his pages of their swords and his footmen of their sticks. And this was the man who, perhaps for the same motives, took a dislike to me simply because I served him well…

I put up with his insults, his viciousness and his ill-treatment patiently, because I thought they resulted from some sort of general unease rather than a personal dislike. But as soon as I realised that he wanted to deprive me of the honour which I deserved for my good service, I decided to resign. The first sign of his dislike for me was the time when he proposed to give a dinner at the embassy to the Duke of Modena and his family, who were visiting Venice; I would not, so his Excellency informed me, be invited to join the table. I replied calmly, but firmly, that as I had the honour to dine there every day, if the Duke of Modena requested that I should not be present at table, it was a point of honour for the ambassador and an absolute necessity for myself that the request should be refused. 'What!' he exclaimed in a rage. 'My secretary, who is not even a gentleman, claims to dine with a sovereign, when my gentlemen do not!' 'Yes, sir,' I replied, 'the post with which your Excellency has honoured me confers such nobility on me for so long as I hold it that I take precedence even over your gentlemen, or those who call themselves such, and am admitted where they cannot go. You are not unaware that on the day when you make your public entry I am required by etiquette and immemorial custom to follow you in ceremonial uniform, and that I then have the honour of dining with you in the Palazzo di San Marco. I do not see why a man who has the right to eat in public with the Doge and the Venetian senate may not eat in private with the Duke of Modena.' My argument could not be faulted, although naturally the ambassador did not give in. In the end it didn't matter, because the Duke of Modena did not come to dinner.

From then on, he never failed to slight me, to mistreat me, and to deny me deliberately the small privileges which accompanied my post, privileges which now belonged to his friend and companion Vitali. And I am certain that if he'd had the nerve to send him to the Senate in my place, he would have done. As well as writing his private letters in his study, the ambassador also got the Abbé de Binis to write M. de Maurepas an account of the Captain Olivet affair, in which, far from mentioning myself or my almost single-handed freeing of the vessel, he even denied me the credit for the interrogatory, a copy of which was included, and attributed it, instead, to Patizel, who had not dared open his mouth. He wanted to annoy me, obviously, and to please his favourites, but he knew that he could not get rid of me, as even he realised that it would not be as easy to find a replacement for me as it was for M. Follau, who had let the world know what he thought of the ambassador. He absolutely needed a secretary who could communicate in Italian well enough to deal with all the answers from the Senate, someone who would write (and cipher, of course) all his dispatches and manage all his affairs in such a way as he would not even have to think about them, and someone with enough sense to serve him faithfully while at the same time, be able to sneak around with his criminal gentleman. Therefore he wanted to keep me, but to quieten me down, keeping me far from my country and without enough money to return in any case. Maybe he would have succeeded if he had gone about it with a little more moderation, but this was something which his advisor, Vitali, did not understand, and his attempts to force me to take action were finally successful. I soon realised that I was wasting both my time and my energy. The ambassador saw my services as crimes instead of being grateful for them, and did nothing but insult me at work and hand me injustices out of it. I thought about my position, and considering the general discredit which he had quite easily managed to bring upon himself, I realised that his hatred might bring me misfortune while his compliments were worth-less. I made up my mind and decided to hand in my notice, giving him sufficient time to find himself a replacement. He ignored my request, and without saying either yes or no, he carried on as before. Seeing that things were not getting any better and were unlikely to do so, and also that he was making no effort to find a replacement, I wrote to his brother and, after setting out my reasons, asked him to obtain my release from his Excellency, adding that whether or not I was granted leave, it was impossible for me to stay any longer. I waited for what seemed like an age for a reply, and I became extremely embarrassed about what I had done. But finally the ambassador received a letter from his brother, which must have been written extremely angrily because, although he was often subject to violent fits of temper, I had never seen him in such a rage before. After showering me with a torrent of obscene abuse, he found himself unable to think of what else to scream next, and ended up by accusing me of selling his cipher. I couldn't believe my ears and burst out laughing, asking him, mockingly, if he thought that there were someone in Venice so stupid as to have given anything for it. This reply threw him into an even more furious rage and he made a big show about calling for his servants to throw me out of the window! Up until then I had been very calm, but when he threatened me in this way, I was also carried away by anger. I rushed to the door and locked it on the inside, preventing his men from entering. 'No, Count,' I said squaring up to him, 'your people shall not interfere in this affair. It shall be settled between us two, if you please.' My actions seemed to surprise him, and he instantly calmed down. When I saw that he had settled, I expressed my feelings with a few well-chosen words then, without waiting for a reply, I opened the door, went out, and walked calmly across the ante-room, past all his servants, who acknowledged me with courtesy, and who I think would have sooner taken my side than their master's. I did not go up to my room but carried on, descending the stairs and leaving the palazzo, never to return.

I went straight to the consul, M. Le Blond, to tell him what had happened. He wasn't that surprised, as he knew both the ambassador and myself, and he kept me for dinner, which although impromptu, was splendid. Every Frenchman in Venice worth speaking of was there, compared with the company which the ambassador kept.

The consul told my tale to the attended guests and when he had finished, everyone agreed on the matter, which was not in His Excellency's favour. As he had not paid me my wages, and as I only had a small amount on me, I was a bit short to pay for my journey home. Everyone chipped in, and I borrowed a generous amount from M. Le Blond, and an equal sum from M. de Saint-Cyr, with whom I was also extremely friendly. I thanked the rest for their generosity and until I left Venice, I stayed with the chancellor of the consulate, as if to prove to the public that not all of the servants of France are as corrupt as her ambassador. Of course, owing to the fact that I was being praised in my misfortune while he, the ambassador, was being ignored, M. de Montaigu completely lost his mind and started behaving like an absolute lunatic. He even went as far as to send a written request to the Senate demanding that I be arrested! The Abbé de Binis warned me about this, and I decided to stay a little longer, rather than leave as I had intended, in order to see the matter out. I was not worried in the slightest – my actions had been witnessed and approved, I was universally respected. The Senate did not even lower themselves to reply to his extraordinary request, and instead sent me a message via the consul saying that I could stay in Venice as long as I liked, and shouldn't worry myself with the rantings of a madman. I carried on seeing my friends, and went to say goodbye to the Spanish ambassador, who received me very graciously, and also the Count Finochietti, the Neapolitan minister, who unfortunately was not at home, but who sent an extremely courteous reply to my letter. Finally I departed, and despite my own financial difficulties, I left no debts other than the loans which I have just mentioned and some money owed to a merchant called Morandi, which Carrio said he would settle for me and which I have never repaid him, although we have met often since then. As for the two loans, I repaid them as quickly as possible.

It would be wrong to leave Venice without a word on her famous amusements, or at least the very small part which I encountered during my stay. It must seem obvious from the direction of my youth how little attention I paid to those things which are thought the pleasures of that age. My tastes did not change in Venice, but my duties, which would have prevented that anyway, made

the small pleasures which I allowed myself all the more
sweet. The most enjoyable of these was simply the company of my friends, men of distinction, M. Le Blond, M.
de Saint-Cyr, Carrio, Altuna, and a charming man from
Friula whose name, I'm embarrassed to admit, escapes
me, although I never remember him without pleasure
and emotion. Of all the men that I have met in my entire
life, he was the one whose heart was most like my own.
We were close, also, to two or three Englishmen, who
were witty, well-educated, and as passionate in their love
for music as ourselves. Every one of these gentlemen had
their wives, or girlfriends, or mistresses, and nearly all
these were at home in places where there was singing
or dancing. There was some gambling too, but very little;
our refined tastes, our collected talents and the theatre
made this seem a very poor option, and it remains, in
my opinion, simply a resource of the bored. I had also
brought with me from Paris the national prejudice
against Italian music, but thankfully, I had also received
from Nature that degree of sensitivity which renders
prejudice powerless. Consequently, I soon acquired the
passion which it inspires in all those fortunate enough

to be born to understand it. When I listened to those barcarolles, I realised that I hadn't heard singing until that moment, and I soon became so possessed by the opera that I couldn't stand all the talking and eating in the boxes and would often sneak off to some other part of the theatre where I would shut myself up all alone, and would submit myself to the pleasure of enjoying the performance to its very end. One day, during such a performance at the Teatro di San Crisostomo, I fell asleep, and far more deeply than if I had been at home in bed. Even the loud and brilliant arias did not awake me, but who could describe the delicate sensations inside me as a result of the delicious harmonies and angelic singing of the song which finally did! What a way to wake up, what ecstasy which opened my ears and eyes together! At first I thought I had awoken in Paradise. This wonderful piece, which I still remember and will do so as long as I live, began:

> Conservami la bella
> Che si m' accende il cor.

I bought the music, and kept it for a long time, but it was not the same on paper as it was inside my head. The notes were the same, but it was not the same thing. That divine aria can only be performed in my head, as indeed it was on that day when I first heard it.

One type of music, which I find superior to the operatic, is that of the *scuole*. The *scuole* are charitable institutions set up for the education of disadvantaged young women, who subsequently receive dowries from the State either when they marry or when they enter a religious order. Amongst all the talents which are cultivated in these young girls, music is considered the most important and every Sunday, in the churches of each of the four *scuole*, motets are sung during vespers, composed and conducted by the greatest masters in Italy for full choir and orchestra, and sung by these girls, the oldest of whom is under twenty, from behind grilled galleries. I cannot believe that there is anything so intensely pleasurable, or so profoundly moving, as that music. The richness of the artistry, the delicacy of the singing, the beauty of the voices, the sensitivity of the execution – everything about those wonderful concerts combines to produce an effect which may not be fashionable, but against which I doubt any man's heart is immune. Neither Carrio nor myself ever missed a single one of those vespers in the Mendicanti, and we were not the only ones. The church was always full of music-lovers, and even singers from the opera came here to learn a thing or two. But what really frustrated me were those infernal grilles, which let me hear those angels – for the singing was worthy of angels – but which prevented me from seeing them. My mind became obsessed and soon I could talk of nothing else. It was during this time, while talking of these girls at his house, that M. Le Blond replied, 'If you are so curious to see these young girls, it is quite easy to satisfy you. I am one of the directors of the institution, and I will take you to tea with them.' I couldn't believe my ears, and pestered him continuously until he managed to arrange it. As we were about to enter the room where I would meet the girls I had dreamt of for so long, I felt such a strong sense of desire that I was almost ill. M. Le Blond introduced me to these famous singers one after another, whose names and voices were all that I had known of them. 'Come,

Sophie' … She was hideous. 'Come, Cattina' … She only had one eye. 'Come, Bettina' … She was deformed by smallpox. There was hardly one of them without something hideously wrong with them. Le Blond could not help but laugh at my reaction. Two or three of them, however, were all right, but they only sang in the choir. I couldn't believe it! We teased them a little during tea, and they became quite animated, and I realised that just because one does not possess beauty, it does not mean that one is also deprived of a sense of grace. 'No one can sing like that without a soul,' I kept repeating to myself. 'They have souls.' In the end, my view of them had changed so much that by the time I left, I was almost in love with every one of the plain creatures. I didn't dare attend their vespers again, but I felt that the worst had passed. I continued to find their music an utter delight, and their voices gave their faces such a charm in my imagination that so long as they continued to sing, I couldn't help but find them beautiful, despite what my own eyes had shown me to be the case.

Music costs so little in Italy that there is no reason to go without it. I hired an instrument, and for a small amount I had four or five performers in my room with whom I practised pieces which I had liked at the Opera. I also had them try some of the orchestral parts from my 'Gallant Muses'. I'm not sure whether it was because he really liked them, or because he wanted to flatter me, but the ballet master of San Crisostomo asked me for a couple of them. I had the pleasure of hearing them played by that wonderful orchestra, and danced to by a very pretty little girl called Bettina, who was kept by one of our friends, a Spaniard called Fagoaga, at whose house we often spent an enjoyable evening.

Speaking of women, Venice is not the sort of place where a man normally goes without. 'Have you no confessions to make here?' I hear someone ask. Yes, I do have some things to say, certainly, and I will tell you about them with the same frankness which I have shown throughout my confessions.

I have always found prostitutes disgusting, and in Venice I had few other women within my reach, the majority of houses within the city being closed to me because of my position. M. Le Blond's daughters were gorgeous, but difficult to approach. And I respected their parents too much even to think about them.

There was one young lady who I found particularly attractive, Mlle. de Catineo, who was the daughter of the King of Prussia's agent, but Carrio was in love with her, and there was even some talk of marriage. He was also well-off and I was broke. He must have earned over twice as much as myself, and not only did I not want to tread on his toes, but I knew that nowhere, and especially Venice, can you start playing the bigshot with as little money as I had. I had not given up my almost ritualistic practice of self-abuse, and I was really too busy to think too much about other temptations. So for more than a year I lived as I had in Paris, and when I left Venice, after eighteen months, I had only approached the opposite sex twice, and then as a result of special occasions, which I shall now describe.

The first was provided to me by *mio amico intimo* Vitali, some time after I forced that public apology from him. There was some discussion at the table one evening about the fun to be had in Venice, and some of those present were getting at me about my supposed indifference to it, declaring that the Venetian courtesans had no equal anywhere in the world. Vitali then said that I must meet the most beautiful of them all, offering to introduce me to her and swearing that she would more than please me. I burst out laughing at his offer, to which Count Peati, a wise, elderly man, remarked with less subtlety than I would have expected that he thought that I was brighter than to be taken to a woman of this sort by an enemy. Still, I will never hope to understand my desires and, against my head, my heart, and my will, I let them drag me off to her out of embarrassment, weakness and, as they say, *per non parer troppo coglione*. We arrived at the house where the *padoana* was very good-looking, even beautiful, although not exactly my type. Vitali left us, and I ordered *sorbetti*, asked her to sing, and after half an hour, put some money on her table and turned to leave. She must have had a strange pride in her work, because she refused to accept money that she had not earned, and I was stupid enough to give in to her. I returned to the palace so convinced that I must have caught something that the first thing I did was to call for the doctor to prescribe some drugs. I cannot begin to describe the unease which I felt over the next three weeks, although I felt no discomfort and had not begun to show any obvious symptoms. I just couldn't imagine that anyone could emerge from the embraces of a *padoana* clean. The doctor himself had a hell of a time trying to convince me and only managed it in the end when he told me that my penis was such an unusual shape, that it was almost impossible for me to catch an infection. I may have kept myself from those dangers more than most, but the fact that I have never once been afflicted by such an attack convinces me, at least, that the doctor was right. I must also say that if I have been blessed with this advantage, I have never gone out of my way to abuse it.

My other adventure was very different both in how it came about and how it ended, although it was also with a woman. I have already mentioned that Captain Olivet, whom I succeeded in helping earlier, gave me dinner on board as a gesture of thanks, and that I took the Spanish secretary with me. I expected a cannon salute as we boarded his ship, but although the crew lined up to receive us, nothing happened, which annoyed me more on account of Carrio, who I could see was rather hurt. It was certainly true that merchant vessels were used to giving a salute of cannon to considerably less important guests than ourselves, and besides, I felt that I deserved it after all that I had done for the captain. I find it impossible to hide my feelings, and although the dinner was very good and Olivet was a generous host, it put me in a real mood, and I ended up eating little and speaking less.

I expected the shots to ring out at the first toast, but nothing. Carrio, who could read me like a book, laughed when he saw me sulking like a child. Just after the first course, I saw a gondola approaching the ship. 'Good lord, sir,' said the captain, 'Look out for yourself. Here is the enemy.' I asked him what he meant, but he just laughed. The gondola came alongside us, and I saw this dazzling young thing leap out, very flirtatiously dressed and extremely lively. In three bounds she was in the state-room and before I had noticed, a place was set for her and she was sitting beside me. She was as charming as she was animated, a brunette of no more than twenty, whose Italian accent alone would have been enough to make her attractive. As she sat eating and chattering, she looked at me, stared wildly, and exclaimed: 'Holy Virgin! Oh, my dear Brémond, what an age since I have seen you!' Then she threw herself at me and started to kiss me furiously, squeezing me so tightly that I almost passed out. Her large, dark Oriental eyes shot right through me, and though I was stunned at first, I soon got so carried away that in spite of the spectators, she had to restrain me herself. When she saw that she had got me to the state that she had intended, she became more modest in her actions, although no less lively, and then began to explain the real, or pretended, reason for her advances. She told us that I was the spitting image of M. de Brémond, the Director of Customs for Tuscany, and that she was still madly in love with him. She had left him like a fool, she said, but would take me in his place. I must also love her as long as she did me, and that when she left, I should bear my disappointment as well as Brémond had done. No sooner said than done, and she took me as though I were hers, giving me her gloves, her fan, her head-dress and her *cinda* to hold. She ordered me about, telling me to do this and that, and of course I obeyed. She told me to send back her gondola because she wanted to share mine, and I did. She told me to swap places with Carrio because she had something to say to him, and I did. They whispered together for a long while, and I said nothing before she called me back. 'Listen,' she said to me, 'I do not want to be loved in the French fashion. Indeed, it would be of no use. The moment you get bored, go. But do not stop half-way, I warn you.' After dinner we went to the glass works at Murano where she bought lots of trinkets and didn't think much to letting us pay for them. Everywhere, her tips were larger than our actual bills, and it became obvious by the way in which she had us throw our money about, that it had no value for her. When she asked to be paid, for example, it seemed to have less to do with greed than vanity, as though her self-respect increased with the amount that was paid for her. In the evening we went back to her rooms, and while we talked, I noticed two handguns on her dressing table. 'Ah,' I said, picking one up, 'here is a vanity box of a new manufacture. May I ask what it is used for? For I know that you have other arms which fire better than these.' We carried on joking for a while and then she told us, with a naïveté which made her even more attractive: 'When I confer favours on men I do not love, I make them pay for the boredom they cause me. Nothing could be fairer. For though I endure their caresses I do not care to endure their insults, and I shall not miss the first man who treats me with disrespect.'

As I left, I arranged to meet her the next day. I couldn't wait, and didn't keep her waiting. When I arrived, she was *in vestito di confidenza*, an erotic state of undress which is unusual except in southern lands, and which I will not attempt to describe here, though I can picture it only too well. I will only say that her frills were edged with a silk thread decorated with rose-coloured tufts, which only seemed to highlight the delicious beauty of her fine skin. I noticed later that this was the fashion in Venice, and its effect is so wonderful that I am surprised that it has not spread further. I had no idea of what was in store for me. I have written, elsewhere, of previous girlfriends with the desire that their memories still arouse in me, but how awful they were compared to my Giulietta. You can't even begin to imagine the effect of that girl, you wouldn't even come close. Virgin girls are no fresher and beauties from a harem no more athletic! Never had such sweet pleasures been offered to a man, and I only wished that I knew how to enjoy it for even a second! Even when faced with such erotic possibilities, I somehow managed to ruin them, as though I were doing it on purpose. It seems that I'm not made for sensual delight and though I carry around the desire for it within me, I also carry the means with which to destroy it.

If there is one incident in my life which, more than any other, reveals my character, it is the one which I am about to describe. I must now remind myself of my reasons for writing this book, so that I may have the strength to prevent myself being overcome by false modesty, which would destroy my attempts. If you have ever wished to know a man, then have the courage to read the next few pages and you will have complete knowledge of myself.

I entered her room as though it were the source of all love and beauty; when I saw her, I felt as though I was in the presence of something divine. I would never have thought it possible to feel any of the emotions which she provoked in me, and respect also. It was as though recognising her beauty, and the delight of her caresses, I tried to take it quickly, all at once, rather than lose it in time. Then suddenly, rather than the fire which I felt inside me, a deathly cold began to fill me and, legs trembling and almost fainting, I sat down and began to cry like a baby.

Who would have guessed why I was crying, or would have had any idea of what was going through my head at that moment? 'This thing which is at my disposal,' I said to myself, 'is Nature's masterpiece and love's. Its mind, its body, every part is perfect. She is not only charming and beautiful, but good also and generous. Great men and princes should be her slaves. Sceptres should lie at her feet. Yet here she is, a wretched street-walker, on sale to the world. The captain of a merchant ship can dispose of her. She comes and throws herself at my head, at mine although she knows I am a nobody, although my merits, which she cannot know, would be nothing in her eyes. There is something incomprehensible about this. Either my heart deceives me, deludes my senses and makes me the dupe of a worthless slut, or some secret flaw that I do not see destroys the value of her charms and makes her repulsive to those who should be quarrelling for possession of her.' I was so convinced of this that I began to look for this fault, with such a persistence that it did not occur to me that the clap might have something to do with it. The softness of her skin, her bright colouring and the sweetness of her breath so completely put any idea of that out of my mind that it was I, still worried about my own health after my visit to the *padoana*, who thought that I may not be clean enough for her.

These strange thoughts brought me almost to tears, and Giulietta, who was obviously not used to having this effect on a man, was unsure of what to do. She walked round the room and looked at herself in the mirror, realising as I did that a lack of beauty had nothing to do with my unusual behaviour. She didn't find it difficult to cheer me up, however, and just as I was about to descend upon her breast, which seemed that it was about to be touched by a man's hands and lips for the first time, I noticed that she had a deformed nipple. I couldn't believe my eyes! I rubbed my eyes and stared further, holding both breasts so that I could check that this nipple did not match the other. Then I began to wonder what had brought about this deformation. I was convinced that this was the result of strange perversion of Nature, and after thinking about this for a short while, it became as clear as day that instead of holding in my arms a creature of unimaginable beauty, I was instead embracing some kind of freak, a monster rejected by Nature, men and love. I became so obsessed by these stupid ideas that I even began to question her about her nipple, and she made a joke of it with such a delightful humour that it was almost enough to paralyse me with love. But I couldn't shake the thought of it from my head, and she couldn't help but notice this, and in the end she began to blush and cover herself up, taking a seat by the window and not uttering a word. I tried to sit next to her, but as soon as I approached her, she got up and sat on the couch, moving again a moment later to walk around the room, fanning herself furiously. Finally she turned to me and exclaimed: 'Lascia le donna, e studia la matematica.'

Before I left, I tried to arrange to meet her the next day, but she put me off till the day after, sarcastically remarking that I must need a rest. The time dragged, my heart full of her and tormented by my strange behaviour and the waste I had made of the time which should have been the most precious of my life. I couldn't wait to make up for it when I saw her, although I had difficulty in reconciling the height of my desires for her with the lowliness of her profession. I hurried to meet her, and although I couldn't guarantee to satisfy her passion on this visit, I could, at least, flatter her pride. I looked forward to the delirious pleasure I would have in showing her the many ways I could make up for my previous performance, or lack of it. In any case, she spared me the trouble. When I arrived at her rooms, I was told that she had left for Florence the previous evening. If I didn't fully appreciate my love for her when she was in my arms, I certainly did now that I had lost her. This unbearable regret has never left me. Though she was beautiful and charming I could just about put up with losing her. What I cannot bear is that she left with only bad thoughts of myself.

So, these are my two stories. I've nothing else to tell about my year in Venice apart, perhaps, for a little scheme we had. Carrio, who was a bit of a ladies' man, got a little fed up with having to go and visit women who were owned by others and decided to get one of his own. As we were the best of friends he suggested an arrangement, which is not unusual in Venice, that we should share one between the two of us. I agreed, and the next question was simply to find a safe one. He became very excited by the idea and managed to find a little girl of eleven or twelve, whom her disgusting mother wanted to sell. We went to visit her together and I couldn't help but pity this poor child, whom you never would have guessed was Italian, as she was so fair and gentle. Anyway, living is cheap in Venice and we gave the mother some cash and made some arrangements for the girl's upkeep. She had a beautiful voice and we gave her a small keyboard and arranged for a music teacher. All this cost us hardly anything, and would save us more in other expenses although as we had to wait until she matured a little, we would have to sow a lot more before we could reap, if you know what I mean. However, we didn't mind going and spending our evenings with her, chatting and playing, and we probably had more fun than if we had

had her there and then. After a while, I became rather fond of our little Anzoletta, although my affections were becoming increasingly paternal, so that my feelings of desiring this girl soon disappeared. If I had approached this girl, it would have felt as though I were committing incest, a feeling which Carrio also began to share. We were receiving a great deal of pleasure from this girl, although it was quite different from that which we imagined when we first layed our eyes upon her. I am certain that no matter how beautiful she would become, it is far more likely that we would have protected her innocence, rather than have corrupted it.

'Rousseau's text … prefers being suspected of lie and slander rather than of innocently lacking sense.'

Paul de Man

NEW WRITING SERIES

CONFESSIONS
Jeremy Millar
Published by Book Works in an edition of 1,000 copies
1996
© Jeremy Millar and Book Works
All rights reserved
ISBN 1 870699 21 1

Book Works would like to acknowledge financial support
from the London Arts Board

New Writing Series
Editor Michael Bracewell

Designed by Rose-Innes Associates
Cover design by Susanne Laws and Jeremy Millar
Printed by Aldgate Press

Book Works
19 Holywell Row
London EC2A 4JB